The Wizard of Oz

by
L. Frank Baum

adapted by
Deidre Laiken

Illustrations by
Pablo Marcos Studio

MOBY BOOKS

Published by Playmore Inc., Publishers,
230 Fifth Avenue, New York, N.Y. 10001
and Waldman Publishing Corp.,
570 Seventh Avenue, New York, N.Y. 10018

CONTENTS

About the Author

Lyman Frank Baum was born on May 15, 1856, in Chittenango, New York. He began his writing career as a teen-age reporter for the *New York World*. Within two years, he was the publisher of a small town newspaper in Pennsylvania.

As a young man, Baum also acted in road companies and wrote plays. One of his musical comedies was produced in New York. He returned to journalism in 1880. Lyman Baum married and had four sons. He settled in Chicago where he founded a trade journal, which helped him to support his family while he continued writing fiction.

The Wizard of Oz, which was first published in 1900, became so popular among its readers that Baum wrote thirteen sequels to the original story. In addition, he wrote books for girls under the pen name of Edith Van Dyne. L. Frank Baum died in 1919.

Characters You Will Meet

Dorothy   *the girl who is whisked by the cyclone to the land of Oz*

Toto   *her dog*

Aunt Em and Uncle Henry   *they hid in the cellar and never left Kansas*

Characters in the Land of Oz

The Wonderful Wizard of Oz

Dorothy's three friends
The Scarecrow
The Tinman
The Cowardly Lion

The four Witches
The Wicked Witch of the East
The Good Witch of the North
The Wicked Witch of the West
The Good Witch of the South

The Munchkins

The Queen of the Field Mice and All the Field Mice

The Guardian of the Gate to the Emerald City

The Winkies

The Leader of the Wolves and the Pack of Wolves

The King Crow and the Wild Crows

The Swarm of Bees

The Monkey King and the Band of Winged Monkeys

The Bending Trees

The China People in the Dainty China Country

The Hammer-Heads

The Quadlings

The Tiny House on the Prairie

Chapter 1
The Cyclone

Dorothy lived with her Aunt Em and Uncle Henry on a small farm in Kansas.

Their tiny house stood alone on a large, flat prairie. Dorothy had only one friend, her dog Toto. He was a small black dog who loved to jump and play.

One day while Dorothy and Toto were playing, they heard the awful sound of a storm. The wind roared and the dust blew smoky circles in the air. Dorothy was frightened.

Uncle Henry stopped working and shouted, "There's a cyclone coming, run for the cellar!"

A cyclone is a terrible storm. Even little Toto wanted to run away. He jumped from Dorothy's arms, ran into the house, and hid under the bed. Dorothy followed him into the house. Then a strange thing happened. The house turned around and around. Then it rose through the air! Toto ran out from under the bed and barked loudly.

It was very dark and the house swayed back and forth. Dorothy held Toto in her arms and listened to the wind. She was frightened. Aunt Em and Uncle Henry were safe in the cellar. She was all alone. Hours passed. The house tossed and turned in the storm. Finally Dorothy closed her eyes and fell asleep.

A Cyclone Is a Terrible Storm.

A Magical Land

Chapter 2
The Munchkins

After a long time, Dorothy woke up. Everything was very quiet. Bright sunshine came through the windows. Toto pressed his cold nose against Dorothy's face. "Where am I?" asked Dorothy. "What happened to Uncle Henry and Aunt Em?"

She ran to the door and looked out at a magical land. All around her were beautiful green trees and colorful flowers. Tiny purple birds sang as they flew from tree to tree. Dorothy had never seen such a lovely place.

Suddenly she heard a small voice say,

"Welcome to the Land of the Munchkins."

Dorothy turned around and there were three men and one woman standing in a circle. They were all the same size as Dorothy, but they looked like grown-ups. They wore hats that rose to a small point about a foot above their heads. Tiny bells tinkled when they moved. The men wore strange blue suits and had long white beards. The woman wore a long gown covered with stars. She made a bow, and in a sweet voice said, "How can we thank you for killing the Wicked Witch of the East? You have set us free!"

Dorothy was shocked.

"There must be some mistake," she said. "I have not killed anyone."

The tiny woman pointed to the house.

"Look, your house landed on the Witch. Those are her feet sticking out from under a block of wood."

"Oh dear!" cried Dorothy. "I'm so sorry."

The Munchkins

"There is nothing you can do," said the woman. "She was a very wicked Witch, and she made the Munchkins slaves for many years. Now thanks to you, we are free!"

"Are you a Munchkin?" asked Dorothy.

"No," answered the woman. "I am the Good Witch of the North."

Dorothy had never heard of a good witch. But the kind woman explained that Dorothy was now in the Land of Oz. In the Land of Oz there were four witches. The witches who lived in the North and South were good witches, and the people loved them. But the witches who lived in the East and West were wicked.

"Now you have killed the Wicked Witch of the East," explained the gentle woman. "There is only one Wicked Witch still alive."

Now Dorothy understood. She was happy to have helped the Munchkins, but she wanted to return to Kansas and see her Uncle Henry

The Good Witch of the North

and Aunt Em.

The Good Witch and the Munchkins had never even heard of Kansas. Dorothy was a long, long way from home. She began to cry. She felt very lonely in this strange land.

When the Good Witch saw that Dorothy was crying, she took off her cap and balanced the point on the end of her nose. She counted to three. The cap changed into a slate. On the slate were the words, "Let Dorothy go to the Emerald City."

Dorothy dried her tears.

"You must go to the Emerald City. Maybe the Wizard of Oz can help you," said the Good Witch.

"Who is the Wizard of Oz?" asked Dorothy.

"He is a great Wizard," answered the Good Witch.

"He is more powerful than all of us put together. He lives in the Emerald City. Only he can help you return to Kansas."

"One—Two—Three."

"How can I get to the Emerald City?" asked Dorothy.

"You must walk," answered the Good Witch. "You will see a Yellow Brick Road. Follow that road and you will find the Wizard of Oz."

Then the Good Witch kissed Dorothy on the forehead. It was a magical kiss, and it left a round, shining mark. It would protect Dorothy on her long trip. The Munchkins gave Dorothy the silver slippers that the Wicked Witch of the East had worn. They had a special magic, but no one knew what it was.

Dorothy put on the silver slippers, waved good-bye to her new friends, and she and Toto began their journey to the Emerald City.

The Magical Kiss

The Scarecrow

Chapter 3
The Scarecrow

Dorothy and Toto followed the Yellow Brick Road for many miles. After a while, they stopped beside a big cornfield and sat down to rest. Not too far away, Dorothy could see a Scarecrow. It was placed high on a pole so it would scare the birds away from the ripe corn. The Scarecrow's head was a small sack stuffed with straw. Someone had painted its face with eyes, a nose and a mouth. It was dressed in a blue suit and wore old boots and a pointed blue hat.

While Dorothy was looking at the Scarecrow,

she was surprised to see one of the eyes slowly wink at her. Then the figure nodded its head in her direction. Dorothy walked up to the Scarecrow.

"Good day," said the Scarecrow.

"Did you speak?" asked Dorothy.

"Certainly," answered the Scarecrow. "How do you do?"

"I'm pretty well, thank you," replied Dorothy. "How are you?"

"I'm not feeling well," said the Scarecrow. "This pole is stuck up my back, and I can't get down."

Dorothy reached up and lifted the figure off the pole. Since the Scarecrow was made of straw, he was very light.

"Thank you very much," said the Scarecrow. "I feel like a new man."

All this seemed very strange to Dorothy. She had never seen a stuffed man who could walk and talk.

Dorothy Lifts Him Off the Pole.

"Who are you and where are you going?" asked the Scarecrow.

"My name is Dorothy," she said, "and I am going to the Emerald City to ask the Great Oz to send me back to Kansas."

But the Scarecrow had never heard of the Great Oz or the Emerald City. Sadly he explained to Dorothy that since his head was stuffed with straw he had no brains. Dorothy felt very sorry for the unhappy Scarecrow.

"Do you think," he asked, "that if I go to the Emerald City with you, the Great Oz will give me some brains?"

"I cannot tell," she answered, "but you may come with me if you like. If Oz will not give you any brains, you will be no worse off than you are now."

The Scarecrow nodded his head in agreement and joined Dorothy and Toto on their journey to the Emerald City.

Setting Off for the Emerald City

"Shall We Go There?"

Chapter 4
The Tinman

After a few hours, the road began to get rough. Walking grew difficult, and the Scarecrow fell many times. But since he was made of straw, he never got hurt.

Soon the daylight faded away and the sky grew very dark. Dorothy could not see at all, but the Scarecrow said he could see in the dark just as well as in the light. Dorothy asked him to stop when he saw a house, for she was becoming very tired.

After a little while, the Scarecrow stopped:

"I see a cottage built of logs and branches.

Shall we go there?"

"Oh yes!" answered Dorothy. "I am really very tired."

When they reached the cottage, Dorothy fell fast asleep with Toto beside her. The Scarecrow, who never needed to sleep, stood in a corner and waited for morning.

As the sun came up, Dorothy was wakened by an awful groan. The sound seemed to come from somewhere in the forest. Dorothy saw something shining not far from where she stood. When she walked deeper into the forest, she saw a remarkable thing. Standing beside a large tree was a man made completely of tin. He held an axe in his hand. Dorothy looked at him in amazement.

"Did you groan?" she asked.

"Yes," answered the Tinman.

"I've been groaning for a long time, but no one has ever come to help me."

"What can I do for you?" asked Dorothy.

A Man Made Completely of Tin

"Get an oil can and oil my joints," answered the Tinman. "They are so rusty I cannot move."

Dorothy ran back to the cottage and found an oil can. The Tinman told her where to put the oil. In just a few minutes the Tinman was able to move.

"How can I ever thank you?" he said. "I might have stood in the forest for years if you hadn't saved me. How did you happen to be here?"

Dorothy explained that she, Toto and the Scarecrow were all on their way to the Emerald City to see the Great Oz. When she told him this, the Tinman began to think.

"Do you suppose Oz could give me a heart?" he asked. "The Wicked Witch of the East cast an evil spell on me as I was out here chopping wood. She turned me into tin and took away my heart."

Dorothy thought for a moment.

Oiling the Rusty Joints

"Why, I think so," she answered. "It would be as easy as giving the Scarecrow brains."

So the Tinman picked up his axe and his oil can and joined his new friends on their journey to Oz.

The Tinman Joins His New Friends.

Toto Barks at the Lion.

Chapter 5
The Cowardly Lion

As Dorothy and her friends continued on their way through the forest, they heard a terrible roar. The next moment, a great Lion ran onto the road. Dorothy and her two friends were very frightened, but little Toto ran ahead and barked at the huge beast.

When the Lion saw the little dog, he opened up his mouth as if to bite him. Dorothy became so angry at this that she rushed forward and slapped the Lion on the nose.

"Don't you dare bite Toto!" she shouted.

"You ought to be ashamed of yourself, a big Lion like you, trying to bite a little dog!"

"I didn't bite him," said the Lion, as he rubbed his nose with his big paw.

"No, but you tried to," Dorothy answered. "You are nothing but a coward!"

The Lion hung his head in shame. He confessed to Dorothy and her friends that although he was supposed to be King of the Beasts, he really was a coward. Large tears fell from his eyes as he told the travelers his sad story. The poor Lion was afraid of almost everything and everybody.

The Scarecrow stopped for a moment and scratched his straw head. Then he said:

"I am going to the Emerald City to ask the Great Oz to give me brains. Maybe Oz could give you courage."

The Lion wiped away his tears.

"If I only had courage, then I could truly be King of the Beasts."

"If Only I Had Courage."

So Dorothy, the Scarecrow and the Tinman invited the Lion to join them on their journey to the Emerald City. The Lion agreed, and the friends continued to follow the Yellow Brick Road towards the home of the Great Oz.

They Follow the Yellow Brick Road.

The Field of Scarlet Poppies

Chapter 6
The Deadly Poppy Field

That night, Dorothy and her friends camped under a large tree in the forest. The Tinman cut some wood with his axe so that Dorothy could make a fire. The Lion hunted for food, and the Scarecrow searched for nuts and berries.

After several days, they passed through the forest and came to a lovely, sunny land. The first thing they saw was a large field of scarlet poppies. Poppies are beautiful flowers, but when there are many of them together, the smell is so powerful that anyone who breathes it falls asleep. Dorothy did not know this, and in a very short time her eyes grew heavy and she sat down to rest.

The Tinman tried to awaken Dorothy. He shouted:

"There is no time to rest. We must hurry and return to the Yellow Brick Road before dark."

But by this time Dorothy was fast asleep. Since the Tinman and the Scarecrow were not made of flesh, the scent of the poppies did not make them sleepy.

"What shall we do?" asked the Tinman. "How will we ever get back on the road to Oz? If we leave Dorothy here she will surely die."

The Scarecrow had an idea. He told the Lion to run quickly through the field, so that he could escape the deadly flowers. Then he and the Tinman could carry Dorothy and Toto out of the poppy field.

There Is No Time to Rest.

So the Tinman and the Scarecrow made a chair with their hands and carried Dorothy slowly through the field.

After a while, they came to a bend in the river. There, lying fast asleep in the flowers, was the Lion. The smell from the poppies had been so strong that the huge beast had given up and fallen asleep.

The Scarecrow and the Tinman felt very sad. Since they could not carry the Lion because he was so heavy, they had no choice but to leave him there to sleep.

Carrying Dorothy Through the Field

A Large Yellow Wildcat

Chapter 7
The Queen of the Field Mice

The Scarecrow and the Tinman sat beside a river and waited for Dorothy to wake up.

"We can't be far from the Yellow Brick Road now," said the Scarecrow. "But which way do you suppose it is?"

The Tinman was about to answer, when he heard a low growl. He turned his head and saw a large yellow wildcat come running towards him. Its mouth was open, showing two rows of ugly, sharp teeth. Its red eyes glowed like balls of fire. It was chasing a tiny grey field mouse. Although he had no heart, the

Tinman knew it was wrong for the wildcat to try to kill such a tiny creature.

So the Tinman raised his axe, and as the wildcat ran by, he gave it a quick blow and cut the beast's head off.

"Oh, thank you, thank you ever so much for saving my life," said the field mouse in a squeaky voice.

"You are quite welcome," answered the Tinman. "Even though I have no heart, I am careful to help those who need a friend, even if it happens to be only a mouse."

The tiny mouse looked shocked.

"Why, I am the Queen—the Queen of all the Field Mice. And since you have saved my life, I owe you a good deed in return."

But the Tinman could not think of anything this tiny mouse could do to help him.

Just then the Scarecrow got an idea.

"I know something you could do to help us," he shouted. "Our friend, the Lion, is fast

The Queen of the Field Mice

asleep in the poppy field. Do you think you could help us move him?"

The Tinman could not understand how a tiny mouse could move a great Lion. But the Queen of the Field Mice informed him that she was queen of thousands of mice. She gave a signal, and in a few minutes they were surrounded by field mice. They came from all directions. There were big mice, and little mice, and middle-sized mice. Each one brought a piece of string in its mouth.

The Tinman and the Scarecrow worked very quickly, and in no time at all, they made a truck out of tree branches. They slowly tied one end of each piece of string around the neck of each mouse and fastened the other end to the truck. When all the mice had been harnessed to the truck, they were able to pull it quite easily.

The Tinman and the Scarecrow sat on the wooden truck while the tiny mice pulled

Each Mouse Brings a Piece of String.

them into the poppy field.

They soon found the Lion. They finally managed to get him on the truck, but they had to work very hard, for the Lion was very heavy. Then with the help of the Scarecrow and the Tinman, the mice were able to pull the truck out of the poppy field.

By this time, Dorothy and Toto were awake, and they were very happy to see their friend the Lion being pulled away from the deadly flowers.

The Queen of the Field Mice bowed and in a squeaky voice said:

"Good-bye, and if you ever need us again, come out into the field and call, and we shall hear you and help you any way we can— good-bye."

Hard Work!

The Gates of the Emerald City

Chapter 8
The Emerald City

The next morning as soon as the sun was up, Dorothy and her friends started on their way. Soon they saw a beautiful green glow in the sky.

"That must be the Emerald City," said Dorothy.

As they walked, the green glow became brighter and brighter. It seemed that at last they were at the end of their long journey.

Finally, they reached the end of the Yellow Brick Road. Before them stood a huge gate covered with emeralds. The jewels glittered in the sun.

Next to the gate was a bell. Dorothy rang the bell, and the big gate swung open very slowly. Inside was a large room covered with shining emeralds. A little man stood inside the room. He was dressed all in green. At his side was a large green box. He asked Dorothy and her friends why they had come to the Emerald City.

"We came here to see the Wizard of Oz," said Dorothy.

The man was so surprised at this answer that he sat down to think.

"It has been many years since anyone has come to see the Great Wizard," he said. "I hope that your business is important, because if you have come here for a foolish reason, he might get angry and destroy all of you."

But the Scarecrow assured the man that they had come on very important business. Then the small man explained that he was

"Why Have You Come Here?"

the Guardian of the Gate, and only he could take them to see the Great Oz. But before they could enter the wonderful city, everyone had to put on green glasses. The Guardian of the Gate explained that the glasses would prevent them from being blinded by the brightness of the Emerald City. He carefully unlocked the box and fitted everyone, even little Toto, with a pair of green glasses. Finally, they were all ready to enter the gates of the Emerald City.

Green Glasses for Everyone

Green Candies! Green Cookies!

Chapter 9
The Great Oz

Even though their eyes were protected by the green glasses, Dorothy and her friends were dazzled by the wonderful city. The streets were lined with beautiful houses which were all made of green marble and covered with sparkling emeralds.

There were many people—men, women and children, all dressed in green clothing. Several shops were open and Dorothy saw that everything in them was green. There were green candies, green cookies, and even glasses of green lemonade. Everyone seemed happy and comfortable in the Emerald City.

The Guardian of the Gate led them through the streets until they came to a big building, exactly in the middle of the city. This was the Palace of Oz. In front of the door stood a soldier. He was dressed in a green uniform and had a long green beard.

"Here are the strangers," said the Guardian of the Gate, "and they demand to see the Great Oz."

The soldier asked everyone to follow him inside the palace. Then he asked them to wait while he brought their message to the Great Oz.

They had to wait a long time before the soldier returned. When he finally came back, Dorothy asked:

"Have you seen Oz?"

"Oh, no," answered the soldier. "I have never seen him. But I spoke to him as he sat behind a screen. I gave him your message.

A Soldier

He said that he will talk to each one of you. But he will only see one of you each day. So you must stay here at the Palace for a few days. I will show you to your rooms."

The next morning, a young woman dressed all in green came to see Dorothy. She gave Dorothy a lovely green dress and even tied a green bow around Toto's neck. Then the woman led Dorothy and Toto to the Throne Room of the Palace to see the Great Oz himself.

After waiting for a few minutes, a bell rang. Dorothy walked into the Throne Room. The room was very big, and all the walls were covered with glistening emeralds. In the middle of the room stood a huge throne. It was shaped like a chair and sparkled with gems. In the center of the chair was an enormous Head. There was no body, or arms or legs to support the Head. It stood alone.

Dorothy looked at the enormous Head with

A Green Bow for Toto

wonder and fear. The eyes in the Head turned slowly and the mouth moved. Then a voice said:

"I am Oz the Great and Terrible. Who are you and why are you here?"

Dorothy was frightened, but somehow she had the courage to answer.

"I am Dorothy, and I have come to ask you to help me return to my home in Kansas."

The eyes looked at her for a few minutes, then a voice said:

"Where did you get those silver shoes, and what is that mark on your forehead?"

Dorothy explained that the shoes had belonged to the Wicked Witch of the East, and that the mark on her forehead was the magical kiss of the Good Witch of the North.

The eyes looked at her carefully. They winked three times, and they turned up to the ceiling and down to the floor and rolled around so they could see every part of the

The Enormous Head

room. Then the Great Oz was ready to give his answer:

"If you want me to help you return to Kansas, you must first do something for me. You must kill the Wicked Witch of the West."

Dorothy began to cry.

"I have never killed anything willingly," she explained. "And even if I wanted to kill the Wicked Witch, I would not know how."

But the Great Oz only said:

"That is my answer. Until the Wicked Witch dies, you will not return to Kansas. Remember that the Wicked Witch is very evil and ought to be killed. Now go, and do not return until she is dead."

Sadly, Dorothy left the Throne Room and told her friends what had happened. The Scarecrow, the Tinman and the Lion felt very sad, because they could not help Dorothy.

The next morning, the soldier with the green beard led the Scarecrow into the

"You Have to Do Something for Me!"

Throne Room. There sitting on the sparkling throne, was a Beautiful Woman dressed in green silk and covered with jewels. Large green wings grew from her shoulders.

The Scarecrow bowed and the Beautiful Woman said:

"I am the Great Oz. Who are you and what do you want?"

The Scarecrow was very surprised. He had expected to see the Head Dorothy had told him about. But he answered the Great Oz and explained that what he wanted more than anything else was to have brains.

Oz was quiet for a few minutes. Then he said:

"I never grant favors without something in return. If you will kill the Wicked Witch of the West, I will give you the best brains in all the land. You will be the wisest man there is."

The Scarecrow was confused.

The Beautiful Woman

"But you asked Dorothy to kill the Wicked Witch of the West," he said.

"So I did," answered Oz. "I don't care who kills her, but until she is dead, I will not grant your wish."

The Scarecrow returned to his friends. He told them that the Great Oz had appeared in the form of a Beautiful Woman but had refused to give him any brains until the Wicked Witch was killed.

The next morning, the Tinman was called into the Throne Room. This time the Great Oz appeared as a Terrible Beast. The creature was as big as an elephant and had a head like a rhinoceros. It had five arms and five long legs. Thick woolly hair covered its huge body. The Tinman had never seen such a terrible creature.

"I am Oz the Great and Terrible," spoke the Beast. "Who are you and what do you want?"

The Terrible Beast

The Tinman explained that he wanted a heart, so that he could love.

Oz waited only a minute before he replied. He explained to the Tinman that he would receive a wonderful heart only if he helped Dorothy and the Scarecrow kill the Wicked Witch of the West.

The Tinman bowed his head and slowly left the Throne Room. When he returned to his friends, he sadly told them what Oz had said.

The next morning it was the Lion's turn to talk to the Great Oz.

When he entered the Throne Room, he expected to see the Great Head, the Beautiful Woman, or the Hideous Beast. But the Lion saw none of these. Instead, to his surprise, he saw a great Ball of Fire. The Ball of Fire was so fierce and glowing that he could hardly look at it. As the Lion moved away from the heat of the fire, he heard a quiet voice say:

"I am Oz the Great and Terrible. Who are

A Fierce, Glowing Ball of Fire

you and what do you want?"

The frightened Lion answered:

"I am a cowardly Lion, afraid of everything. I came to beg you to give me courage so that I can become King of the Beasts."

The Ball of Fire burned for a time, and then the voice said:

"Bring me proof that the Wicked Witch is dead, and then I will give you courage."

The Lion was angry at the Great Oz, but he was too frightened to say anything. So he ran from the room and joined his friends.

After the Lion told Dorothy what had happened, she looked at him sadly.

"What shall we do now?" she asked.

"There is only one thing we can do," answered the Lion, "and that is to go to the Land of the Winkies, where the Wicked Witch lives, and destroy her."

"But suppose we can't destroy her?" said Dorothy.

The Lion Runs from Oz.

"Then I will never have courage," said the Lion.

"And I will never have a heart," said the Tinman.

"And I will never have brains," said the Scarecrow.

"And I will never see Aunt Em and Uncle Henry," cried Dorothy.

The four friends thought for a long time.

"I suppose we must try it, but I am sure I do not want to kill anybody, even to see Aunt Em again," said Dorothy.

So Dorothy and her friends decided to begin their journey the very next morning.